O9-AHV-650

SADDLEBACK
EDUCATIONAL PUBLISHING

think green

Alternative Fuels

ISBN-13: 978-1-59905-348-6
ISBN-10: 1-59905-348-9
eBook: 978-1-60291-676-0

Printed in Guangzhou, China
0410/04-206-10

13 12 11 10 2 3 4 5 6 7 8 9

Contents

Alternative Fuels: An Introduction

Fuels are substances that when burned or consumed produce energy. For example, car engines burn gasoline to produce energy. Most fuels in use today are derived from petroleum. Fuels that are not derived from petroleum are known as *alternative fuels* because they provide an alternative source of energy. Alternative fuels include natural gas, propane, hydrogen, biofuels, alcohol, and other fuels. Other sources of alternative energy include solar energy, hydro (water) energy, and wind energy.

Global Energy Crisis

Energy consumption in the world has been growing steadily since the industrial revolution. Most of this energy comes from the burning of fossil fuels like petroleum. Each year millions of vehicles are bought around the world. The majority of these vehicles run on petroleum. In the United States, there are an estimated 230 million vehicles, and that number continues to grow every year. This creates an ever-increasing demand for petroleum. The demand will soon exceed supply. This gap will continue to grow as new vehicles are added to the world's roads and highways. Since fossil fuels are nonrenewable sources of energy, this will create a global energy crisis in the near future.

Vanishing Resources

Nonrenewable energy resources cannot be easily replaced by nature once they are used up. Nonrenewable resources such as coal, oil, and natural gas take millions of years to form naturally. They are therefore in limited supply. These resources are found inside the Earth in solid, liquid, or gaseous form. Petroleum is found in liquid form, coal is solid, and natural gas and propane are gases. The continuous use of these nonrenewable resources is making them slowly vanish from our planet.

The Need to Go Alternative

The increase in global energy consumption has led to a higher demand for energy resources like petroleum. With limited supply, most countries have to import petroleum to meet their energy needs. In the United States, petroleum provides about 40% of all energy needs. However, the burning of petroleum emits large amounts of greenhouse gases such as carbon dioxide. This poses a threat to the environment and contributes to global warming. A possible solution to the problem is to use alternative fuels and invest in natural renewable energy resources.

Why Alternative Fuels Are Better

Replacing conventional fuels like petroleum with alternative fuels helps reduce greenhouse gas emissions. For example, a compressed natural gas (CNG) vehicle emits about 60% to 90% less smog-producing gas, while liquefied petroleum gas (LPG) vehicles emit 30% to 90% less carbon monoxide. This makes alternative fuels safer and cleaner for the environment. The use of other renewable resources such as solar energy, hydro energy, and wind energy is also an easy way to go alternative.

Renewable Energy

Renewable energy resources are natural resources that can be formed and replaced by nature in a short period. Nature is forming these resources constantly. Renewable resources include plants, animals, soil, water, and sunlight. Minerals such as salt or clay are also renewable resources, as they are abundant in nature.

Did you know?

Until the 1950s, the United States produced nearly all the petroleum it needed. In 2000, to meet growing demands, 11 million barrels of petroleum was imported every day.

Vegetable Oil

Vegetable oil is a renewable alternative fuel that can be used to run diesel engines. Vegetable oil is obtained from plants such as corn, soybean, peanut, safflower, sunflower, palm, etc. It is therefore nontoxic, biodegradable, and eco-friendly. Vegetable oil is also one of the most affordable alternative fuels.

Why vegetable oils?

Vegetable oil, a commonly available alternative fuel, provides environmental, economical, and health benefits. Burning vegetable oil does not emit sulfur dioxide, the main component of acid rain. The superior lubricating properties of vegetable oil provide a smoother running engine with less noise. Increased use of vegetable oil has led to an increased demand for vegetable oil crops, thus benefiting the farmers.

Vegetable Oil Limitations

Vegetable oil is thicker than conventional oil. It must be clean and hot. It also needs to be filtered before use. In the winter, vegetable oil does not work properly. Vegetable oils are unreliable at both high and low temperatures. The major drawback of vegetable oil is that it reduces engine life. It is also more expensive than gasoline and diesel.

How to Use Vegetable Oil Properly and Safely

- Mix the vegetable oil with diesel fuel or kerosene and then use.
- Blend vegetable oil with an organic solvent additive or gasoline and then use.
- Use vegetable oil in a properly installed two-tank system. The oil is first preheated and then used.

Extraordinary Vegetable Oil

Soaking your finger in vegetable oil for a few minutes can remove a splinter. The oil can separate stuck glasses, remove labels and stickers from plastic and glass jars, and can even soften your feet. Vegetable oil also helps in controlling mosquito growth in still water. Pour a few tablespoons of oil onto the water surface and keep mosquitoes away.

Vegetable Oil Versus Petroleum

Compared to petroleum, vegetable oil releases:
- 100% less SO_2
- 78% less CO_2
- 48% less carbon monoxide
- 48% less asthma-causing particulate matter
- 80% fewer cancer-causing hydrocarbons

Vegetable Oil Extracted Per Acre of Crop

- Soybean: 40 to 50 gallons/acre
- Rapeseed: 110 to 145 gallons/acre
- Mustard: 140 gallons/acre
- Jatropha: 175 gallons/acre
- Palm oil: 650 gallons/acre
- Algae: 10,000 to 20,000 gallons/acre

Did you know?

Vegetable oil improves gas mileage by over 3% and reduces smog-forming nitrogen oxide emissions by 75% when used as motor oil.

Peanut Oil

Peanut oil is a clear oil made from crushed peanuts that can be used as an alternative fuel in diesel engines. Peanut oil is a nontoxic, safe, clean, biodegradable, and eco-friendly alternative fuel. In 1900, German engineer and inventor of the diesel engine Rudolf Diesel first used peanut oil as a fuel for his diesel engines. This was the first time that peanut oil was used as an alternative fuel to run diesel engines.

U.S. Peanut Production

In 2007, the estimated production of peanuts was 3.74 billion pounds, which is 8% more than in 2006. Peanuts are produced in the U.S. southeast, Virginia and the Carolinas, and the southwest. The production of peanuts requires well-drained, light-colored, friable, loose soil with high levels of calcium and moderate levels of organic matter.

Disadvantages of Peanut Oil

Peanut oil is more expensive than other alternative fuels. Peanut oil freezes at extremely high temperatures because of its high pour point. *Pour point* is the temperature at which oil no longer flows like a liquid. Peanut oil can also soften and degrade parts of an engine. When not perfectly mixed, peanut oil increases nitrogen oxide emissions.

New Peanut Variety

At the University of Georgia, scientists are trying to develop nonedible peanuts with high oil content grown specifically for biodiesel production. The production of high oil content peanut varieties would not pose a risk to peanuts grown for cooking purposes in the world market.

Peanut Biodiesel and Fossil Fuel–Based Biodiesel

Peanut biodiesel is compatible with fossil fuel–based biodiesel. They can be mixed in any proportion. Peanut oil shows a 2% to 5% reduction in miles per gallons compared to fossil fuel–based biodiesel, which can be overcome by altering diesel engines.

Rudolf Diesel

Rudolf Diesel was an inventor and engineer. In 1892, he invented the diesel engine, which was named after him. He was interested in using vegetable oil or coal dust as fuel in his engines. He developed the first engine that ran on peanut oil and demonstrated it at the World Exhibition in Paris in 1900.

Wood

Wood is a major source of heat and light and one of the oldest fuels in use today. Wood is also used as an alternative fuel in steam engines and turbines to generate electricity. Wood has many advantages as an alternative fuel, as it reduces carbon dioxide emissions and therefore causes less pollution. It is also a commonly available renewable resource.

Types of Wood Fuel

- *Logs* are the most common and simplest form of wood fuel. They are used as a domestic fuel in open fires and stoves for heating water and cooking.
- *Wood chips* are primarily used as a fuel in commercial-scale boilers. Commercial-scale boilers are used to heat large buildings such as factories, hotels, and offices.
- *Wood pellets* are small, compressed pieces of wood produced as a byproduct of sawmilling. Pellets have very low moisture content and burn efficiently. They can be used in anything from domestic pellet stoves to very large boilers.

Did you know?

A unit of wood fuel is called a *cord*. One cord of wood fuel gives about 22,000,000 Btu (British thermal units) of heat, which is second only to coal.

Why use wood fuel?

Wood is a renewable resource and emits less carbon dioxide into the atmosphere. Wood fuel is cheaper compared to the costs of fossil fuels. It provides opportunities for new companies to develop sources of income and employment, especially in rural areas. Neglected woodlands can be managed properly and can provide habitat for wildlife. Local production of wood fuel can reduce the transportation costs.

Wood and the Environment

As compared to fossil fuel, wood fuel has many environmental advantages. The amount of carbon dioxide produced during the burning of wood is less in comparison to fossil fuel. The smoke from burning wood is relatively nontoxic to the environment. Wood fuels reduce the amount of airborne sulphur and heavy metals, which contribute to acid rain.

Wood in Africa

People in most parts of Africa use wood as one of the most important forms of domestic energy. For example, in the Giyani area of the Limpopo province in South Africa, 80% of the villagers use wood as the only energy source for cooking and heating.

Wood in Europe

In Europe, some countries like Sweden and Austria use wood to generate electricity. Sweden produces 1,490 megawatts of electricity from wood, and Austria produces 747 megawatts. In Finland, people use wood waste, such as pellets, as domestic and industrial sources of energy. Scandinavian countries import firewood from Baltic countries such as Lithuania and Latvia. The cost of manual labor is cheaper in these countries in comparison to Scandinavian countries.

Biodiesel

Biodiesel is an alternative fuel that is made from vegetable oils or animal fats combined with alcohol. Biodiesel can be used as an alternative fuel in diesel vehicles with few or no modifications. In the United States, most biodiesel is made from soybean oil. Many manufacturers make biodiesel from used oils, fats, and even grease. Biodiesel can be used in its pure form or mixed with diesel in various proportions.

Why biodiesel?

Biodiesel is an environmentally friendly, biodegradable, and nontoxic alternative fuel. It burns cleanly and produces fewer pollutants such as carbon monoxide, particulates, hydrocarbons, etc. Biodiesel is sulfur-free and thus reduces the sulfur levels in the diesel supply. It also smells better and produces less black smoke.

Producing Biodiesel

Oils or fats are raw materials from which biodiesel is made. First, the oils or fats, which are hydrocarbons are filtered and then mixed with an alcohol like methanol. A catalyst such as sodium or potassium hydroxide is then added to speed up the chemical reaction. The final product from the chemical reaction is a biodiesel fuel.

Heating Oil

Biodiesel as a heating oil is gaining popularity. Several types of domestic and commercial boilers are using biodiesel as a heating fuel. Many Americans are also using biodiesel as a substitute for household heating oil. Increasing prices of conventional heating oil have also helped increase demand for biodiesel.

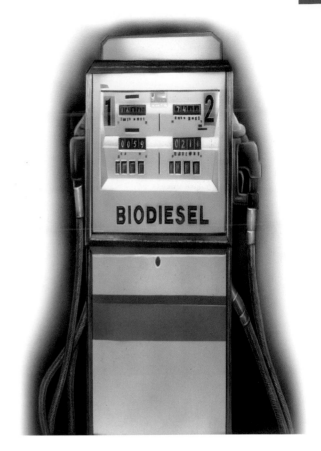

Labeling Biodiesel

The letter "B" along with a number is used to designate biodiesel fuel. The number represents the percentage of biodiesel in the mixture of biodiesel and petroleum. For instance, a mixture of 40% biodiesel and 60% petroleum is labeled *B40*. The most commonly used biodiesel fuel is *B20*.

Biodiesel Versus Fossil Fuels

Compared to fossil fuel, biodiesel releases:
- 50% less hydrocarbon
- Fewer sulfur oxides and sulfates
- 50% less carbon monoxide
- 75% to 85% fewer cancer-causing compounds

Did you know?

According to the National Biodiesel Board, the United States is producing around 75 million gallons of biodiesel annually.

Biomass

Biomass is organic material derived from plants and animals that can be used as a fuel. It is a clean and renewable energy resource that can be found all over Earth's surface. Biomass can also be converted into other forms of energy such as heat and electricity.

Applications of Biomass Energy

- Biomass is used as an alternative source of energy. Cattle dung is used in India to produce biogas, which is used in cooking.
- The leftovers of a biogas plant are used as fertilizer.
- Leftovers from sugar mills are sold after extracting juice from sugarcane, which is known as *bagasse*. Bagasse is used as a biomass to run electricity-producing turbines.
- Wood, the most abundantly found biomass, is used for room heating and cooking.
- Biomass is used in homes for fireplaces, hot water heating, and space heating, as well as in industries for electricity generation.

What is biomass made of?

- *Wood residues* are the remains of wood derived from woodlands and commercial forests. They include wood chips, slabs, edgings, sawdust, and shavings.
- *Agricultural residues* are obtained from farming activities. They include crop residues, vegetable or food-processing residues, and livestock slurry.
- *Energy crops* are purposely grown to serve as a source of biomass. They include herbaceous grasses, short-rotation tree crops, and cereal crops.

Did you know?

One pound of dry plant tissue can produce energy equivalent to a half pound of coal.

How much biomass is used for energy today?

Biomass is the fourth-largest source of energy after coal, oil, and natural gas. Surveys estimate that biomass is used to generate about 35,000 megawatts (MW) of electricity around the world. About 7,000 MW of that is used in the United States alone. Most of the biomass is used in heat and power systems for the pulp and paper industries. Only 7% of the annual biomass production is used by the total world population.

Why use biomass?

Biomass helps in reducing global warming. It emits a lower amount of carbon dioxide and sulfur dioxide, which cause acid rain. The use of biomass reduces the demand for petroleum imported from other countries. Biomass is also used in producing ethanol, which can be used in environmentally friendly cars.

Biomass Materials Used to Produce Electricity

- Leftover sawmill wood
- Leftover paper and wood waste from paper mills
- Farm waste such as corn stalks, corn cobs, and seed corn
- Paper and cardboard that cannot be recycled
- Fast-growing crops and trees

Wind Energy

Wind energy is a form of energy obtained from moving air. Wind energy can be converted into other useful forms of energy such as electricity. This makes it an important alternative energy resource.

Wind Generates Electricity

Wind energy has been used to produce electricity for many years. Earlier, *windmills* were used to generate electricity, and now *wind turbines* have taken their place. Windmills have a series of blades, while wind turbines have only two or three blades. When the wind blows, the blades turn. The rotating motion of the blades is converted inside a turbine into an electric current.

Wind Farms

Wind farms are flat, open areas with wind blowing at a speed of at least 14 miles per hour. A wind farm has dozens of wind machines to produce electricity. Wind power is the world's fastest-growing technology for generating electricity. The Horse Hollow Wind Energy Center in Texas is the world's largest wind farm. It has 421 wind turbines that power 230,000 homes per year.

Measuring Electricity Produced by Wind Energy

The electricity measured by wind turbines is measured in kilowatts (kW), megawatts (MW), and gigawatts (GW). The production and consumption of electricity are measured in kilowatt-hours (kWh). A kWh refers to electricity produced or consumed in one hour. Electricity produced by a wind turbine depends upon the size of the turbine and the speed of the wind. A 10 kW wind turbine generates 10,000 kWh in a year with average wind speeds of 12 miles per hour.

Wind and Environment

Wind is considered green power technology. It has no harmful effects on the environment. Wind power plants or wind farms produce no air or water pollution. Wind energy is also not responsible for emitting greenhouse gases and thus does not contribute to global warming.

Limitations

Wind turbines create a swooshing sound, which makes noise pollution. Wind can never be predicted. Despite the most advanced equipment, it is not possible to create wind energy all of the time. Wind turbines create problems with TV transmissions. They also are potentially dangerous to birds, as the moving blades can kill them.

Did you know?

A single 1.5-megawatt wind turbine powers about 300 average American homes, year after year.

Solar Energy

Solar energy is energy derived from the sun in the form of heat and light. The sun is around five billion years old. Humans have been using the sun's energy for thousands of years. Solar energy is used to power vehicles, heat homes, and cook food. In the United States, more than 200,000 homes use solar energy for their heating needs.

Solar Cells

Solar energy is converted into electricity using *solar cells*. A solar cell is also known as a *photovoltaic cell* or *PV cell*. Solar or photovoltaic cells are usually made from silicon alloys. They were developed in the 1950s for use on U.S. space satellites. Now, photovoltaic cells are used in calculators, toys, telephone booths, and watches. Photovoltaic energy can also be used in homes for lights and other appliances.

Advantages and Disadvantages of Photovoltaic Cells

Photovoltaic cells convert solar energy directly into electricity. Photovoltaic cells are easy to install and can be used anywhere. They do not require any heavy mechanical generator systems. Photovoltaic cells do not generate any byproducts or create any noise pollution. The disadvantage of using photovoltaic cells is that they work only in hotter climates. Photovoltaic cells are not useful in cloudy weather or at night.

Environmentally Friendly

Solar energy is a renewable source of energy available to us free of cost. It is environment-friendly and does not have any adverse effects on our environment. The use of solar energy does not emit carbon dioxide and harmful waste products that cause air or water pollution.

Solar Thermal Power Plants

Solar thermal power plants use solar energy to generate electricity indirectly. The solar thermal collectors are fitted to heat a fluid that creates steam. A turbine converts the steam into mechanical energy, which in turn is converted into electricity through a generator attached to the turbine.

Solar Ovens

Solar ovens are one of the most common ways to use solar energy. They are used in cooking, drying, and pasteurization. Balanced fuel costs and reduced firewood demand have made solar ovens popular. Solar ovens also reduce or even remove the smoke in the air and thus improve air quality.

Did you know?

In a year, an average 10-square-foot area of the planet's surface gets energy from the sun that equals nearly a barrel of oil.

Negative Impact

Despite the environment-friendly nature of solar energy, it does have some negative impact on the environment. The manufacture of photovoltaic cells uses silicon and generates some harmful waste products. Mismanaged solar thermal farms can also harm desert ecosystems.

Hydroelectric Power

Hydroelectric power, or *hydroelectricity,* is power that is generated by the force of flowing water. Hydroelectricity is a renewable source of energy. It is one of the cleanest and cheapest sources of energy. Water from rivers, rapids, waterfalls, and dams is used to generate electricity. Rainwater and melting snow can also be used. Hydroelectricity provides about 24% of the total global electricity requirement. In 2005, about 7% of the total electricity needed in the United States was provided by hydroelectricity.

Itaipu Dam

Advantages of Hydroelectric Power

- Hydroelectricity is renewable.
- Hydroelectricity is pollution-free and uses no fossil fuel.
- No greenhouse gases are released by the production and use of hydroelectricity.

Disadvantages of Hydroelectric Power

- Dams often disturb aquatic life.
- Construction of hydropower plants is expensive.
- Dams flood large areas of land, displacing all forms of life from areas where they are built.

How is hydroelectricity produced?

Hydroelectricity is produced at a *hydroelectric power station.* Water is stored in a reservoir or artificial lake behind a dam. When the water is released from the reservoir, it passes through a long pipe known as a *penstock.* The water builds up pressure as it travels through the penstock and falls on the blades of a turbine, which is connected to a generator. The force of the falling water rotates the blades of the turbine, which drives the generator and produces electricity. The world's first hydroelectric power plant, on the Fox River in Appleton, Wisconsin, began working in 1882. The United States now has more than 2,000 hydroelectric power plants.

Aswan Dam

Grand Coulee Dam

Hoover Dam

Famous Dams

Dam	Place
Aswan High Dam	Aswan, Egypt
Edwards Dam	Augusta, Maine
Folsom Dam	Folsom, California
Grand Coulee Dam	Grand Coulee, Washington
Hoover Dam	Arizona and Nevada
Itaipu Dam	Brazil and Paraguay
South Fork Dam	Johnstown, Pennsylvania
Three Gorges Dam	Three Gorges, China
Niagara Dam	Roanoke County, Virginia

History of Hydropower

Hydropower is an age-old source of energy. The Greeks were one of the earliest known users of hydropower. They used water wheels to grind wheat into flour. These water wheels were very similar to modern-day turbines. Large water wheels were used to generate power during the Middle Ages in different types of mills. The modern-day water turbine was developed from the water wheel. It was invented by Benoit Fourneyron, a French engineer, in 1827.

Three Gorges Dam

The Three Gorges Dam on the Yangtze River in China is the world's largest dam. The dam is still under construction and will be ready to operate by 2011. The construction of the dam will benefit many people, but it may also cause serious problems as it will submerge 13 cities, 140 towns, and 1,352 villages and displace 1.9 million people. The dam water will immerse several historical sites and animal species, too.

Top Ten Hydroelectric Power Producing Countries

- China
- Canada
- Brazil
- United States
- Russia
- Norway
- India
- Japan
- Sweden
- France

Did you know?

The Grand Coulee Dam on the Columbia River in the state of Washington is the largest hydroelectric power facility in the United States.

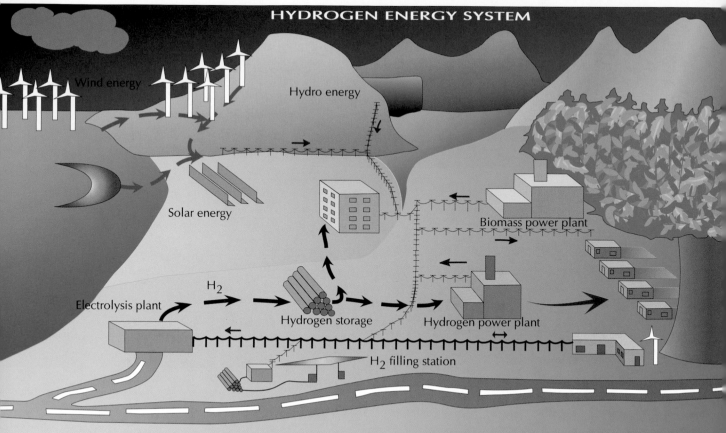

Hydrogen Energy

Hydrogen is a colorless, odorless gas that can be used as an energy source. Hydrogen has many advantages as an alternative fuel. It is one of the most abundant elements found in nature. It is renewable and efficient. Hydrogen reduces greenhouse gas emissions and improves the quality of air.

Sources of Hydrogen

Hydrogen is found almost everywhere on Earth. Hydrogen can be produced from a variety of easily available resources:

- *Primary energy sources:* water, sunlight, wind
- *Traditional or conventional energy sources:* natural gas, gasoline, diesel, propane
- *Renewable/alternative fuels:* methanol, ethanol, landfill gas, biogas, methane
- *Other sources:* ammonia, sodium borohydride, algae, peanut shells

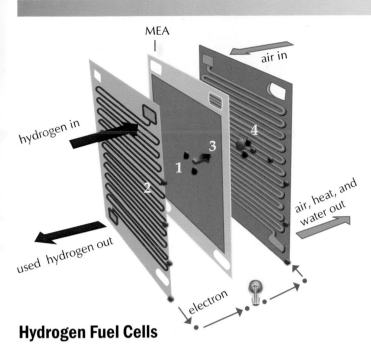

MEA

air in

hydrogen in

used hydrogen out

air, heat, and water out

electron

Hydrogen Fuel Cells

Hydrogen contains chemical energy. A *hydrogen fuel cell* uses this chemical energy contained in hydrogen to generate electricity. A hydrogen fuel cell is very much like a battery. It uses hydrogen and oxygen from the air to generate electricity. A hydrogen fuel cell produces no waste except heat and water. The advantage of a hydrogen fuel cell is that it can provide a continuous supply of energy. A hydrogen fuel cell is safe and produces almost no pollution.

Hydrogen in the United States

Hydrogen is most widely used to generate electricity in the United States. It is commonly used in the metal refining, waste treatment, and food processing industries. It is also used in households and in fuel cells to power vehicles, laptops, and cell phones. The National Aeronautics and Space Administration (NASA) uses liquid hydrogen fuel to launch the Space Shuttle into space. Hydrogen fuel cells provide power to electrical equipment in the Space Shuttle. The states of California, Louisiana, and Texas are leaders in hydrogen production.

Bio-Hydrogen

Bio-Hydrogen is hydrogen produced from biomass or by any other biological process. Dark fermentation reaction is a biological process used to produce hydrogen. Dark fermentation reaction uses bacteria to ferment organic waste, which produces hydrogen.

Did you know?

Hydrogen is the lightest element on Earth, yet it has the highest energy content per unit weight of any fuel.

World's Largest Hydrogen-Powered Electricity Generation Plant

Each year the United States imports 55% of its crude oil. By 2025, imports are expected to rise to 68%. To meet its growing energy needs, the United States is going to build a low-carbon electricity power plant in California. It will be the world's largest hydrogen-powered electricity generating plant. The plant will generate enough energy to supply power to 325,000 homes in southern California.

HydroGen3 Minivan

Hydrogen as an Alternative Motor Fuel

Hydrogen can also be used as an alternative motor fuel. Most vehicles around the world run on internal combustion engines. The biggest advantage of hydrogen is that it can be directly used as a motor fuel in internal combustion engines. Another advantage is that the engines require little modification when hydrogen is used as a fuel. Hydrogen also provides three times the energy per pound of gasoline. However, it has one disadvantage: Liquid hydrogen has one-tenth the density of gasoline. This means that vehicles running on hydrogen need to have larger fuel tanks.

Wave Power

Oceans cover 70% of Earth's surface. They are the largest absorbers of solar energy, which makes them a potential source of clean and renewable energy. Tapping as little as 0.2% of this energy in the oceans could generate enough power to meet all our energy requirements. Ocean energy can be derived from waves and tides.

Wave Power

Waves are a renewable resource for storing solar and wind energy. Waves carry enormous amounts of energy that is released at the coastline. Ocean waves along the world's coastlines can generate up to two to three million megawatts of power. Some wave-power-rich coastlines are found in the western United States, Europe, southern Africa, northern Canada, Japan, New Zealand, and Australia. In the United States, the California coastline has the highest potential for producing wave power.

How are waves formed?

As winds blow over the oceans, they transfer their energy to the surface. Winds create tiny ripples on the water's surface. The tiny ripples become bigger as the wind continues to blow. These small waves turn into bigger waves as the wind grows stronger. The movement of waves depends on the speed of wind—the faster the wind, the faster the waves.

Using Wave Power

Waves can provide an extremely large supply of power. For example, in Europe's Atlantic coastline, nearly 65 megawatts of electricity can be generated from every 0.9 mile of coastline. Power generated from waves is used to generate electricity for industrial and domestic use. Wave power is the chief source of energy used in desalination plants that treat seawater to make it drinkable. It is also used to pump water into reservoirs.

Wave Farms

Wave farms are setups used to generate wave power using different technologies. The world's first wave farm, Aguçadora Wave Park, has been established on the coast of Portugal. The park uses the Pelamis wave energy conversion device to harness wave power. The Pelamis system uses massive red steel tubes linked together. The tubes are connected to a power grid via a single cable to generate electricity.

Destructive Waves

Tsunamis are an example of the enormous energy stored in waves. The Indian Ocean tsunami that occurred off the west coast of Sumatra, Indonesia, on December 26, 2004, left millions homeless in 11 countries. According to the U.S. Geological Survey (USGS), the tsunami released the energy of approximately 23,000 Hiroshima-type atomic bombs.

Salter Duck

The "Salter Edinburgh Duck" was a deepwater apparatus that was devised to capture wave energy. The Duck was designed to match the orbital motion of the waves and generate electricity by moving up and down along with the waves. The Duck was developed in the 1970s by Professor Stephen Salter at the University of Edinburgh in Scotland.

Early Use of Wave Power

Wave power was used as a source of energy in the Middle Ages. During this period, farmers used to trap seawater in millponds and use it to power watermills as the tide dropped. However, with the invention of cheaper and more reliable sources of energy, harnessing wave power declined.

Tidal Power

Ocean tides are moving water masses that rise and fall periodically over most of the Earth. Ocean tides are a potential source of clean, alternative energy. When a tide flows in or out, it carries along with it a large amount of energy. If all tidal energy could be tapped, we would be able to generate about 64,000 megawatts of electricity. However, tides at all coastlines around the world cannot be used to generate electricity. Only coastal areas where the difference between high and low tides is at least 16 feet can be used to generate tidal power. Potential sites for generating tidal power can be found in the United Kingdom, New Zealand, Turkey, Australia, and Canada.

Generation of Tidal Power

Tidal fences, turbines, or barrages are used to generate tidal power. The simplest method of producing tidal power is by constructing a *barrage* or a dam. A barrage has a sluice gate that opens to let water in. This raises the water level in the barrage. When the tide recedes, the water is emptied into a turbine system. The force of falling water rotates a turbine that drives a generator, which produces electricity. *Tidal fences* are turbines mounted vertically on fences, and *tidal turbines* are large heavy turbines similar to wind turbines.

Why use tidal power?

- Tidal power is renewable, reliable, and non-polluting.
- Tidal power produces neither greenhouse gases nor any other waste.
- Tidal power is predictable, as tides occur twice every day.
- Building tidal power plants on the shore may protect coastlines against high storm tides.

Largest Tidal Power Plant

The world's largest tidal power plant is situated at the estuary of the La Rance River in France. It was built in 1966, generates 600 million kilowatt-hours every year, and can supply energy to almost 250,000 homes.

Energy Island

Energy Island is a concept of constructing a floating island capable of generating electricity using renewable sources like waves, ocean currents, wind, and solar energy. The idea of Energy Island is based on the Danish island of Samso, which is self-sufficient in its energy requirements. The island of Samso gets 100% of its electricity from wind power and heat energy from the sun and biomass. It is estimated that 50,000 such energy islands would be sufficient to meet the world's total energy requirements. Along with generating electricity, they could also provide enough drinking water, as a byproduct of the process, for the entire world population.

Highest Tides (Tide Ranges) Around the World

Country	Site	Tide Range (feet)
Canada	Bay of Fundy	53.1
France	Port of Ganville	48.2
England	Severn Estuary	47.5
France	La Rance	44.2
Russia	Penzhinskaya Guba (Sea of Okhotsk)	43.9
Argentina	Puerto Rio Gallegos	43.6
Russia	Bay of Mezen (White Sea)	32.8

Did you know?

The Bay of Fundy in Nova Scotia, Canada, has the highest tides in the world and can produce up to 14,000 MW of tidal power.

Geothermal Power

Earth is also a source of heat energy. Earth's mantle and core produce tremendous amounts of heat. Geothermal power converts hot water or steam from deep inside the planet's surface into electricity. For example, in the United States, the state of California meets most of its electricity demands from geothermal energy. Geothermal reservoirs are usually found near volcano and earthquake sites. Most geothermal reservoirs in the world are located in an area surrounding the Pacific Ocean known as the "Ring of Fire."

Hot Springs

Hot springs are natural springs that have a continuous flow of hot, bubbling water. The water in a hot spring is naturally heated by geothermal energy. Hot springs are found all over the world. Some hot springs are present even under the seas and oceans. Hot springs are geothermal energy resources.

Geysers

Geysers are hot springs that expel fountains of hot water and steam. Geysers are geothermal energy resources. The word *geyser* is derived from the Icelandic term *gjósa*, which means "to gush." Geysers are formed when the pressure of groundwater becomes high due to geothermal heating. For example, thousands of gallons of water are released into the sky every day by the Old Faithful Geyser of Wyoming.

The Geysers Geothermal Field

The Geysers geothermal field in California is the largest geothermal power plant. It is spread over an area of about 120 miles and is the largest dry steam field. The Geysers Field has been generating electricity since 1960. It generates enough electricity to light up more than 22,000 homes. Presently, it supplies electricity to 1.1 million people.

Early Use of Geothermal Energy

Geothermal energy has been used since ancient times for various purposes. The Romans, Chinese, Icelanders, and New Zealanders have used it over the years for heating and cooking. People of many early civilizations used hot water springs for bathing. In North America, geothermal energy was used 10,000 years ago by Paleo-Indians. They used it as a source for cleansing and healing.

Geothermal Power Plants

Geothermal power plants are built near geothermal reservoirs. They are similar to any other power plant except that they do not burn fuels to generate electricity. In a geothermal power plant, cold water is pumped down into the Earth's crust through pipes and the Earth's heat converts the cold water into heat and steam. The steam is used to propel turbines to generate electricity. The heat generated is used directly in heating systems installed in buildings. The Larderello geothermal power station in southern Tuscany, Italy, was the world's first geothermal power station. It was established in 1911. The site of the power station was the *Valle del Diavolo* (Devil's Valley).

Did you know?

Italy's Larderello was the first place in the world to use geothermal electricity, in 1904.

Ethanol and Methanol

Ethanol is a colorless liquid with a distinctive smell. This renewable biofuel is widely used as an alternative fuel. Ethanol is blended with unleaded gasoline and used as a transportation fuel. It is now the most widely used transport biofuel in the world. Ethanol is a cleaner fuel and emits 25% less greenhouse gas than any conventional vehicle fuel. Ethanol is produced by fermenting sugar obtained from crops such as corn, sorghum, sugarcane, wheat, and rice. It can also be produced from grass, vineyard grapes, wood, crop residues, or old newspapers.

Why use ethanol?

- Ethanol does not contain toxic substances like lead and benzene.
- Ethanol is a clean fuel. Ethanol produced from corn can reduce greenhouse gas emissions by 25% as compared to gasoline. Ethanol produced from grass, vineyard grapes, wood, crop residues, or old newspapers can reduce greenhouse gas emissions by as much as 100%.
- Ethanol boosts crop production and contributes to the economy.
- The United States imports 60% of its petroleum from other countries. Ethanol can increase savings over imported oil.

Ethanol in Brazil

Brazil is the one of the world's largest producers of ethanol. Ethanol fulfills about 30% of the country's vehicle fuel requirements. The Brazilian ethanol industry uses mainly sugarcane and cane waste to produce ethanol. Using ethanol has not only helped reduce pollution but also prevents the burning of cane waste. After harvesting sugarcane, most sugarcane farmers would clean their fields of the waste by burning it. However, ethanol industries utilize cane waste, and this prevents air pollution that is created by burning the waste.

Ethanol in the United States

The United States is the largest producer of ethanol. Ethanol in the United States is produced mostly from corn. Most cars in the United States now use a blend of at least 10% ethanol. Ethanol is produced in 20 states. The states of Iowa, Illinois, Minnesota, and Nebraska are the leading producers of ethanol in the United States.

Methanol

Methanol, commonly known as wood alcohol, is obtained from natural gas and biomass like wood and its byproducts, seaweed, and garbage. It can be used as a substitute for gasoline and diesel in cars, trucks, and buses. Methanol is commonly used as a fuel in racing cars.

Why use methanol?

- Vehicles running on methanol emit fewer hydrocarbons and other polluting compounds. These vehicles emit less nitrogen oxide and almost no particulate matter.
- Using methanol would reduce dependence on conventional fuels.
- Methanol provides better acceleration and power to vehicles.
- Methanol is less flammable than gasoline.

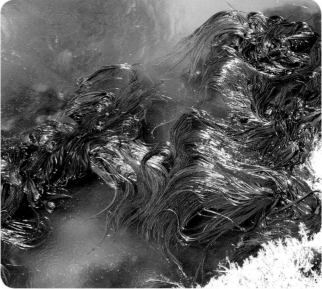

Did you know?

A methanol-based vehicle is $300 to $500 more expensive than a gasoline-powered one.

Natural Gas

Natural gas is a colorless and odorless gas. Like other fossil fuels such as coal and oil, natural gas is found under the planet's surface. Natural gas is made up mostly of a gas called *methane*. Methane is a simple hydrocarbon, made up of hydrogen and carbon. Hydrocarbons are primarily used as a fuel to produce heat and electricity or to power vehicles. This makes natural gas useful for industrial, household, and transportation purposes. About 22% of the total energy requirements in the United States come from natural gas.

How is natural gas formed?

Natural gas is formed from the decayed remains of plants and animals. This decayed plant and animal matter is called *organic material*. Over millions of years this organic material formed thick layers covered by rock and soil. Heat and pressure change these trapped organic materials into coal, petroleum, and natural gas. Natural gas is found near petroleum reserves.

From Underground to Homes

Several natural gas companies work to bring natural gas to our homes. They use big wells and pumps to drill thousands of feet deep inside the Earth to bring natural gas to the surface. They transport the natural gas to towns and cities through gas pipelines buried underground. The gas is sent to homes through small pipes, which are connected to a gas meter that measures the gas usage. Natural gas is mixed with a chemical before being distributed to homes. This gives natural gas a rotten egg smell and makes it easily detectable in case of a leak.

Measuring Natural Gas

Natural gas is measured in cubic feet. The heat stored in a cubic foot of natural gas can be measured in British thermal units (Btu). One Btu is the amount of heat needed to raise the temperature of one pound of water by 1° F. One cubic foot of natural gas has about 1,031 Btu.

Natural Gas Power Plants

Natural gas power plants produce electricity. They are cleaner and more efficient than coal plants. They also emit fewer pollutants. In the United States, natural gas generates 18% of the electricity.

Natural Gas Use in the United States

The following pie chart shows the breakdown of natural gas usage in the United States:

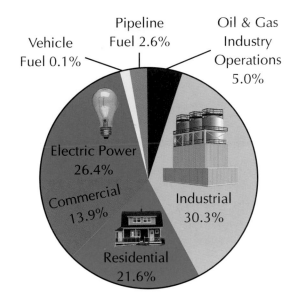

Natural Gas Safety

- In case of a natural gas leak, immediately get out of the house. Natural gas leaks smell like a rotten egg.
- Install a carbon monoxide detector in your home. It detects natural gas and can save lives.
- Keep children away from gas appliances, and put safety covers on the knobs.
- Be careful when working near a gas flame. Do not wear loose clothes, because they can catch fire easily.
- Avoid using gas appliances to keep you warm.
- Do not keep paint or other volatile chemicals near a gas appliance.
- Make sure to have gas appliances checked regularly for any defects.
- Avoid playing around a gas appliance, as the piping may come loose.
- Do not hang on gas pipes. It can loosen them and can cause leakage.

Did you know?

In the United States, there are about one million miles of underground gas pipelines. About 62 million families use natural gas for domestic purposes.

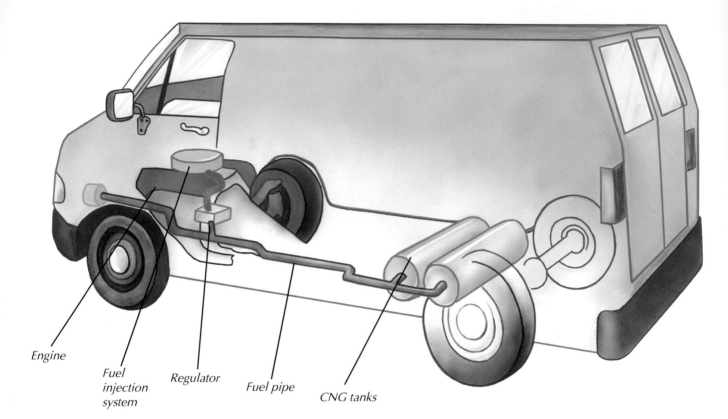

Engine

Fuel injection system

Regulator

Fuel pipe

CNG tanks

Compressed Natural Gas (CNG)

Natural gas can be used as an alternative fuel to run motor vehicles. Natural gas used in vehicles is compressed under high pressure in special tanks called *cylinders*. The compressed natural gas, or CNG, has a lower volume and occupies less space. This makes the size of CNG cylinders more manageable for use in vehicles. CNG is widely used in buses, trucks, and cars. CNG is safe, clean, and one of the least expensive alternative fuels.

Why compressed natural gas?

Vehicles powered with gasoline produce nitrogen oxides, which react with organic compounds and sunlight to form ozone. CNG-powered vehicles are cleaner than gasoline-powered vehicles. These vehicles emit 85% less nitrogen oxide, 74% less carbon monoxide, and 70% fewer reactive hydrocarbons than gasoline-powered vehicles.

Safer CNG

CNG is lighter than air and will rapidly rise into the sky when a leak occurs, so land and water are not contaminated. The ignition temperature of CNG is 1,200° F, double that of gasoline. This makes it flammable only in concentrations from 5.3% to 15%. CNG ignites only when the leak happens in a confined space.

The following table shows the fuel characteristics of CNG compared to gasoline and diesel:

	CNG	Gasoline	Diesel
Toxic to skin	No	Moderate	Moderate
Toxic to lungs	No	Moderate	Moderate
Specific gravity lighter or heavier than air (air = 1.00)	0.55 (lighter)	3.4	4.0
Source/feedstock	CNG	Petroleum	Petroleum

Dos and Don'ts for CNG Conversion

- Check to make sure the CNG workshop is authorized to install CNG kits in your vehicle.
- Do a thorough pre-conversion check for your vehicle.
- Make sure you are using the right kit and cylinder for the particular make of your vehicle. Buy all components from a single source.
- Keep a record of the type of mechanism and precautions of a CNG vehicle, and follow them.

World's Largest Fleet of CNG Buses

The world's largest fleet of CNG buses is owned by the Delhi Transport Corporation in India. The fleet has about 3,106 CNG buses that ply 773 routes on the roads of New Delhi, the capital of India. New Delhi has about 110 CNG stations. CNG buses were introduced in New Delhi in 1998, and all public transport buses were converted to CNG in 2002.

CNG Vehicles

CNG vehicles are widely used for commercial purposes ranging from taxicabs and small trucks to heavy duty trucks like school buses and transit buses. The lower cost of production and storage of CNG makes it a useful alternative fuel.

Did you know?

In 1994, there were about 55,000 CNG vehicles in the United States.

Liquid Natural Gas

Liquid natural gas (LNG) is natural gas that has been liquefied by cooling. LNG is used as an alternative fuel all over the world. The advantage of LNG is that it is a clean fuel and causes no significant harm to the environment. When exposed to air, it evaporates quickly and disperses without leaving any residue. LNG is relatively cheap and easy to transport.

Liquefaction Plant

Liquefaction plants for natural gas follow the same principles used in refrigerators, heat pumps, and freezers. Liquefaction plants have production lines known as *trains*, which remove sulfur compounds, water, carbon dioxide, hydrocarbons, and more from natural gas. Methane remains in the form of gas with small amounts of propane, ethane, and nitrogen. These trace gases are used as a refrigerant fluid. The refrigerant fluid compresses and expands to remove heat from the natural gas. The cooling process goes through several stages until the methane becomes a liquid.

Using LNG

LNG is one of the most widely used alternative fuels in the United States. It is used for heating homes, running vehicles, and generating electricity. LNG has been a reliable fuel for domestic and industrial uses for more than 45 years. More than 64 million American homes use LNG every day.

How is LNG made?

LNG is made by freezing natural gas to −260° F to condense it into a liquid. This process is known as *liquefaction*. Liquefaction makes LNG a pure fuel by removing water vapor, butane, propane, and other trace gases found in ordinary natural gas. This LNG is more than 98% pure methane.

Did you know?

LNG now provides about 2.5% of the annual U.S. natural gas needs. This is expected to grow to nearly 15% by 2025.

Shipping LNG

LNG is shipped in huge, double-walled, stainless steel tanks. Double-hulled ships are used to carry these tanks. A double-hulled ship is generally more than 900 feet long. It uses several insulated pipes to load and unload LNG tanks.

Supply Chain of LNG

Gas field → Liquefaction plant → Storage tank → Shipping → Storage tank → Distribution through pipelines

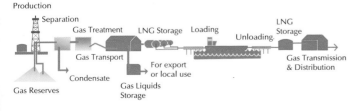

The Worst LNG Accident

The worst LNG accident took place in the United States in 1944. An LNG tank leaked and spilled its contents into the street and sewer in Cleveland, Ohio. The resulting explosion and fire killed 128 people. Investigators found that the LNG steel alloy tank had low nickel content, which made it brittle when exposed to the cold LNG. The tanks had low nickel content because of the shortage of nickel during World War II. Since then, quality materials and procedures are used in LNG facilities.

Compressor Refrigeration

Natural gas is liquefied using a refrigeration process. Michael Faraday's theory was used to develop the process of compressor refrigeration in the 19th century. In 1912, the first plant that used refrigeration to liquefy natural gas was built in West Virginia.

Liquid Petroleum Gas

Liquefied petroleum gas, or LPG, is a mixture of hydrocarbons such as butane and propane. LPG is a gas at normal temperatures but is stored and transported as a liquid by compression or refrigeration. LPG is used as an alternative fuel to power vehicles. Vehicles running on LPG produce fewer toxic and smog-forming air pollutants. It is less expensive than gasoline.

Where does LPG come from?

LPG is obtained from the separation of natural gas products and from refining crude oil. Natural gas products provide 60% of the world's total LPG supply, and oil refining provides the remaining 40%. LPG is found abundantly in the North Sea, which can supply LPG for many years.

Why use LPG?

LPG is a clean and environmentally friendly alternative fuel. It helps in reducing emissions, as LPG vehicles produce less carbon monoxide and fewer nitrogen oxides and hydrocarbons. In comparison to gasoline, LPG contains fewer non-combustible components, thus leaving no residues like acid and carbon deposits. This helps to increase the life of the engine. Vehicles fitted with LPG systems are also secure from fuel theft, as it is not easy to steal fuel from them.

Number of LPG Vehicles by Country

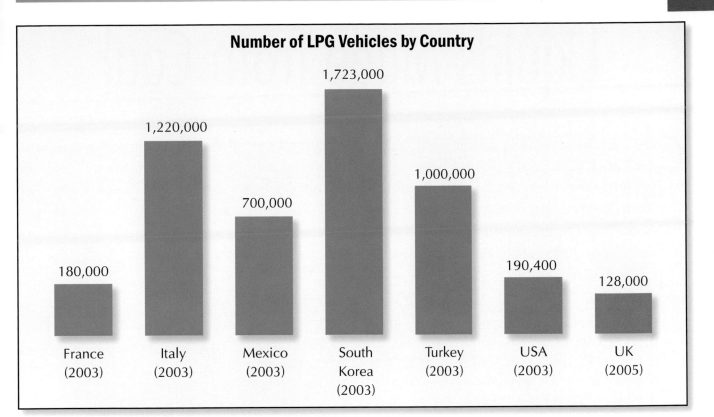

180,000	1,220,000	700,000	1,723,000	1,000,000	190,400	128,000
France (2003)	Italy (2003)	Mexico (2003)	South Korea (2003)	Turkey (2003)	USA (2003)	UK (2005)

Autogas

LPG used in cars is known as *autogas*. Cars running on autogas produce 50% less carbon monoxide, 35% fewer nitrogen oxides, and 50% less ozone. Autogas has been used as an alternative fuel in spark ignition engines since the 1940s in some countries. Today, this nontoxic and non-corrosive fuel is also used in diesel engines. Autogas can cut fuel bills by about 50% and is cleaner and cheaper than gasoline or diesel.

LPG Use Around the World

LPG is used in vehicles around the world. It is estimated that about 8.1% of total LPG is used as a transportation fuel. Almost 90% of taxis in Japan use LPG, including Tokyo, where all taxis run on LPG to reduce urban smog. In South Korea, 1.7 million cars run on LPG, making it the world's largest LPG user. In the United States, LPG is used in fleets, school buses, taxicabs, and police cars.

Did you know?

More than 9 million vehicles in 38 countries run on autogas.

Liquids Made from Coal

Coal can be used as a source for making alternative fuels. The fuels or liquids made from coal are called coal-to-liquid fuels, or CTLs. With the help of modern technology, coal can be converted into clean and zero-sulphur synthetic oils such as gasoline and diesel. Coal is an abundant energy resource that is found in more than 70 countries around the world. According to the World Coal Organization, there is still around 909 billion tons of coal left, which would last for another 100 to 200 years. CTL could answer our search for an alternative domestic fuel.

Why go for CTL?

- CTL can be used in existing conventional engines.
- CTL is free from sulfur and nitrous oxide.
- CTL can reduce carbon dioxide emissions by 20%.
- CTL can help in reducing oil imports.
- CTL is cost-efficient and gives better performance.
- CTL is environmentally friendly.

Uses of CTL

CTLs can be used for:
- Transportation
- Cooking
- Generating power

How is coal converted to liquid fuel?

Coal is usually converted to liquid fuel by what is process known as the *Fischer-Tropsch process*. In this process, coal is converted into a gas called *syngas*, which is condensed to obtain liquid fuel. The Fischer-Tropsch process was developed by German coal researchers F. Fischer and H. Tropsch in 1923. The process was used during World War II to produce oil. In 1944, Germany had 25 coal liquefaction plants, which fulfilled 90% of the nation's liquid fuel requirements.

CTLs Can Save Our Environment

Liquefied coal fuels are biodegradable and environment-friendly. Most impurities and pollutants are removed from coal during the initial steps of production. This prevents the emission of harmful acids or hazardous air pollutants during production. CTLs are cleaner than conventional diesel and gasoline, as they emit far fewer toxic pollutants and nitrogen oxides and less mercury.

Coal Liquefaction in China

China is the second-largest consumer of petroleum in the world, after the United States. The country's petroleum production is much less than its consumption. In 2007, China imported 3.19 million barrels per day. To meet the escalating oil demands and reduce its petroleum dependence, China is exploiting its coal reserves. China has 13% of the world's total coal reserves, which is enough to meet the coal consumption for a century or more. It has invested $6 billion in coal liquefaction plants. The first coal liquefaction plant will start production in 2008 and is likely to produce 50,000 barrels of gasoline daily.

Coal Liquefaction in South Africa

South Africa began production of coal-derived fuels in 1955. It is the only country in the world that is actively producing CTL. The country obtains 30% of its gasoline and diesel from coal.

Coal Liquefaction in the United States

The United States depends on imported petroleum to meet its fuel requirements. In 2005, an estimated 8.322 million barrels per day was produced, while consumption was 20.8 million barrels per day. However, this shortage and dependence on foreign oil can be curbed if the United States opts for coal-to-liquid fuels. The country has the world's largest coal reserves. Converting just 5% of its reserves will help meet the nation's fuel needs.

Did you know?

By 2025, the United States will have to import 70% of its petroleum.

Waste as an Energy Source

Every day tons of waste comes from households and industries. Disposing of waste is a big problem. Waste not only occupies large spaces but also pollutes the environment by contaminating soil, water, and air. This problem can be solved by treating waste to produce a clean source of alternative energy. There are various technologies for treating waste to produce heat and electrical energy. The United States is the fourth-largest converter of waste into energy. About 14% of the country's solid waste is treated to generate energy, which can power nearly three million American households.

Incineration

Energy from waste can be generated by burning. This process is known as *incineration*. Waste is burned at about 1,832° F in waste-to-energy plants. It reduces the waste to 10% of its original volume and produces heat energy that can be used for various purposes.

Anaerobic Digestion

Organic waste such as animal manure and food-processing scraps decomposes by anaerobic digestion to generate biogas. *Anaerobic digestion* uses microorganisms to break down organic waste to produce biogas. *Biogas* is rich in methane and carbon dioxide and can be used to run any type of heat engine or to generate electricity. Biogas is one of the oldest known forms of renewable fuel. It was used as early as the 10th century BCE in Assyria to heat water. The first anaerobic digester was built in Mumbai, India, in 1859.

Landfill Gases Contribute to Global Warming

Landfills release methane and carbon dioxide by decomposing organic waste. Methane and carbon dioxide are potent greenhouse gases that cause global warming. Recovering energy from methane would help us considerably reduce global warming. It would also help decrease the consumption of thousands of tons of coal per year. Landfill gases also contain volatile organic compounds, which are equally dangerous. These gases contribute to the formation of photochemical smog.

Countries Utilizing Maximum Waste

Luxembourg, Sweden, the Netherlands, France, and Denmark utilize maximum waste. Denmark incinerates the highest amount of waste in the world. Every year the country produces about 13 million tons of waste and utilizes 85% to 90% efficiently. Heat generated from waste is used for household heating in 25% of the homes across the country.

Magnegas

Magnegas is a clean gas produced from liquid waste such as sewage and used motor oil, antifreeze, and glycerin by the Plasma Arc Flow process. It is cleaner than other alternative fuels such as natural gas, biodiesel, and ethanol and can be a substitute for natural gas. Magnegas can be used in cars, electric generators, and stoves.

Did you know?

Processing just a ton of waste would generate 1.4 MWh of electricity, 79 gallons of potable water, 11–22 pounds of commercial salt, and 330 pounds of construction material.

Electric Cars

Electric cars are battery-powered vehicles that use an electric motor. They are environmentally sound and cause no pollution. Electric cars can reduce greenhouse gas emissions by almost 98%.

How an Electric Car Works

An electric car is propelled by an electric motor, which is powered by a rechargeable battery, fuel cells, or a generator. The electric motor is controlled by a controller. The controller manages the supply of power. It keeps a check on the inflow of power from the battery and outflow of required power to supply the motor. In one charge, a car can run about 100 miles, and after that it would need recharging.

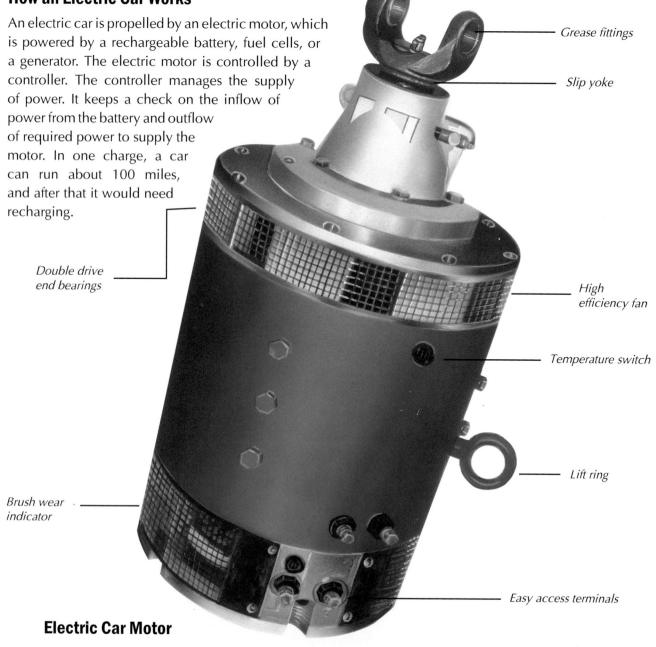

Grease fittings

Slip yoke

Double drive end bearings

High efficiency fan

Temperature switch

Lift ring

Brush wear indicator

Easy access terminals

Electric Car Motor

Advantages of Electric Cars

- Electric cars are clean, 100% emission-free vehicles.
- They use solar or hydrogen fuel cells. They do not use any nonrenewable sources of energy, and thus they decrease our dependence on gasoline.
- They are fuel-efficient. Electric motors convert almost 75% of chemical energy stored in batteries, while internal-combustion engines convert just 20% of energy.
- Electric cars perform better than gasoline-powered vehicles. They are quiet and smooth to operate and require less maintenance.

Development of the Electric Car

The first electric car was a carriage powered by non-rechargeable batteries. Scottish inventor Robert Anderson developed it between 1832 and 1839. In 1839, various kinds of designs and models of electric cars were displayed in an exhibition in Chicago. Not long after, electric cars became quite popular in the United States. In 1900, almost one-third of all cars on New York City, Boston, and Chicago roads were electric cars. However, the development of Henry Ford's Model T, a gasoline-powered car, affected the popularity of electric cars. Gasoline was cheap and easily available. The usage of electric cars became negligible in the United States until Congress passed a bill to promote their usage to reduce pollution in 1966.

Other Electric Vehicles (EVs)

Minivans, sport utility vehicles, pickup trucks, and buses are a few other vehicles that run on batteries like electric cars. Electric vehicles cost more than gasoline-powered vehicles. Nevertheless, they are environment-friendly and safer than gasoline-powered vehicles. Electric vehicles are zero-emission vehicles. Their motors do not produce any exhaust or fumes. In case of an accident, they are less likely to roll over. They do not have a gas tank, which makes them less vulnerable to fire.

Types of EV batteries

- Lead-acid
- Nickel-metal hydride
- Nickel-cadmium
- Lithium-ion
- Zinc-air
- Flywheels

Did you know?

The United States has more than 4,000 electric vehicles.

Fuel Cells

Fuel cells are a clean and renewable source of alternative energy. A *fuel cell* is an electrochemical device that produces electricity by a chemical reaction. Fuel cells combine oxygen with other gases and chemical compounds like hydrogen, methanol, phosphoric acid, potassium hydroxide, and carbonate salt to produce electricity and heat. Fuel cells are used to power cell phones, automobiles, airplanes, and space shuttles.

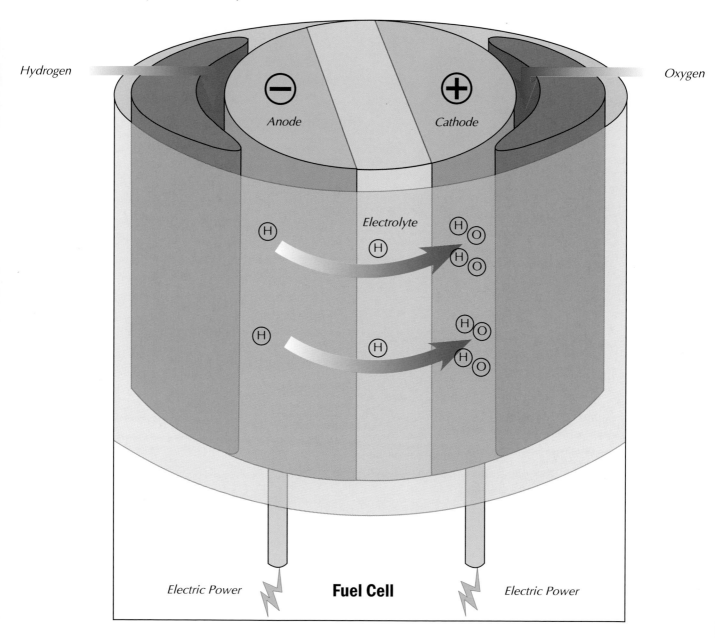

Development of Fuel Cells

Sir William Grove

Sir William Grove, a Welsh judge and scientist, developed the first fuel cell in 1839. In 1959, about 120 years after the first fuel cell was developed, Francis Bacon developed the first practical fuel cell. In the same year, Harry Karl Ihrig built a tractor powered by a fuel cell.

Fuel Cells in Civil Aircraft

Fuel cells can be used to make airplanes more eco-friendly, lighter, and more fuel-efficient. In 2008, the first successful test of fuel cells was done on an Airbus A320 airplane. During the test, hydrogen- and oxygen-based fuel cells generated 20 kilowatts (kW) of electricity to power the airplane.

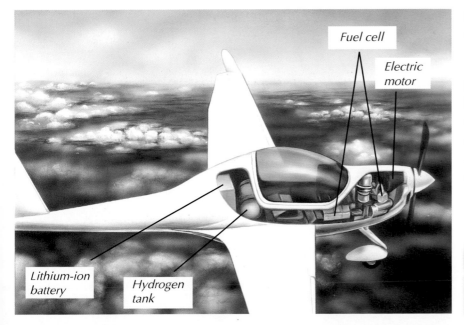

Fuel cell

Electric motor

Lithium-ion battery

Hydrogen tank

Fuel Cells Reduce Carbon Dioxide Emissions

Fuel cells reduce greenhouse gas emissions. Fuel cells used in buses and two-stroke scooters cut down carbon dioxide emissions and reduce noise pollution. They also significantly reduce tailpipe emissions.

Did you know?

Sir William Grove is known as the "father of the fuel cell."

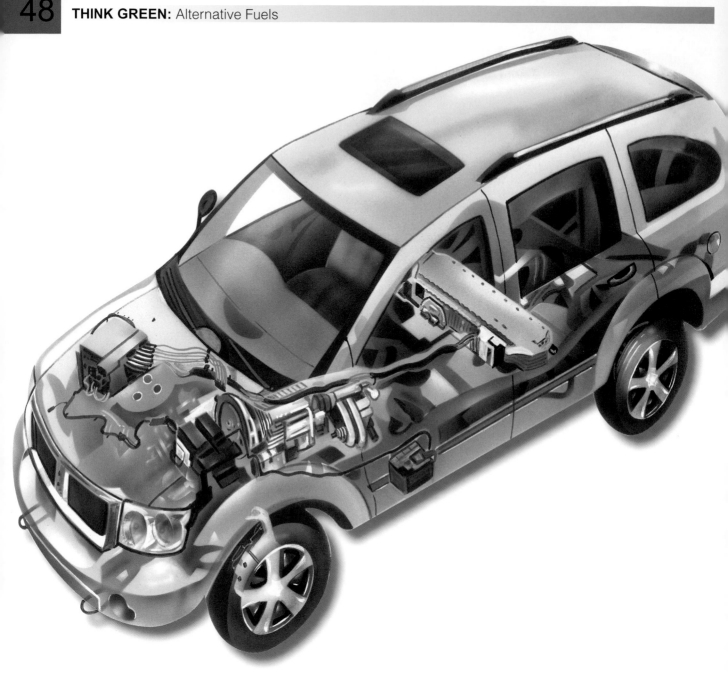

Hybrid Cars

Hybrid cars run on more than one kind of energy. Most hybrid cars combine an internal-combustion engine with an electric motor, which provides better performance and fuel economy. The electric motor assists the engine to accelerate and recharges automatically when the car is being driven.

Types of Hybrid Cars

Hybrid cars can be full hybrids, mild hybrids, or plug-in hybrids. In *full hybrids*, the electric motor helps the combustion engine in propelling the car. When the car is stationary, all car accessories run on the battery. Full hybrids have powerful and long-lasting batteries. At lower speeds, these cars can move on the electric motor alone. *Mild hybrids* are not capable of moving on the electric motor alone. *Plug-in hybrids* are similar to full hybrids. However, unlike full hybrids, plug-in hybrids use an extension cord to recharge their batteries from an electrical outlet.

Reduction of Greenhouse Gases

Conventional-fuel vehicles emit high amounts of greenhouse gases. Hybrid cars substantially reduce greenhouse gas emissions. Studies have shown that if we increase the use of plug-in hybrid cars by 2050 by 60%, this will help us reduce about 450 million tons of greenhouse gases.

Did you know?

There are more than 14 different types of hybrid cars available to U.S. buyers.

Why use hybrid cars?

- Hybrid cars are eco-friendly.
- Hybrid cars are fuel-efficient. They reduce our consumption of fossil fuels and dependence on foreign oil.
- Hybrid cars have idle-off capability. As the car stops or goes idle, the gasoline engine will turn off automatically, preventing waste.
- Hybrid cars have regenerative braking. A lot of energy is lost every time we apply brakes while driving. However, in hybrid cars this energy is not lost. Hybrid cars have a generator that converts this lost energy into electricity and recharges the battery.
- Hybrid cars cause less noise pollution.

Flexible-Fuel Vehicles

Flexible-fuel vehicles (FFVs) are automobiles that can run on gasoline or a mixture of gasoline with methanol or ethanol. Most FFVs are designed to accept blends of ethanol and methanol up to 85%. FFVs cause less pollution than gasoline and diesel vehicles.

FFV Technology

A *flexible-fuel vehicle* is simply a modified model of an existing vehicle. It has only a few modifications in the engine and the fuel system. Like a conventional vehicle, a flexible-fuel vehicle has a single fuel tank, fuel system, and one engine. The difference between a gasoline-fueled vehicle and a flexible-fueled one is a sensor within the fuel system. The sensor is a small computer microprocessor that detects the fuel composition and automatically adjusts the engine's fuel injection and ignition.

E85

E85, or ethanol 85, is a blend of ethanol that contains 85% ethanol and 15% gasoline. E85 is largely used as a fuel in FFVs. In the United States, E85 is largely available in the states of Iowa, Illinois, Minnesota, and Nebraska.

E10

E10 is another alternative fuel that is suitable for FFVs. E10, or ethanol 10, is a blend of ethanol and gasoline that contains 10% ethanol and 90% gasoline. Unlike E85, E10 can be used in any gasoline vehicle made after 1980.

First FFV

In 1908, Henry Ford designed the first flexible-fuel vehicle, a Model T, that operated on either ethanol or gasoline. Earlier, during the 1880s, Ford designed a car that ran solely on ethanol.

Did you know?

Almost 50% of the cars in Brazil and more than six million vehicles in the United States are FFVs.

Benefits of Ethanol Blended Fuels

- E85 is a cleaner fuel and can reduce emissions of greenhouse gases. It emits lower levels of carbon monoxide, carbon dioxide, nitrogen oxides, and ozone-forming volatile organic compounds than gasoline.
- Ethanol-based fuels are comparatively cheaper than gasoline.
- Ethanol-based fuels reduce dependence on fossil fuels.

Human-Powered Vehicles

Human-powered vehicles are the most eco-friendly form of transportation. Human-powered vehicles are driven by manual power. In early times, humans used muscle power to drag and pull vehicles such as sledges and carts. In 1418, Giovanni Fontana made the first human-powered vehicle. The vehicle had four wheels and used a long rope passing through gears to the wheels.

Why human-powered vehicles?

Despite the increasing demand for motor vehicles because of their speed and convenience, human-powered vehicles are still used in most parts of the world. Human-powered vehicles continue to be used because of their low cost and sustainability. They do not use renewable energy sources and therefore cause little or no air pollution. Human-powered vehicles are environmentally friendly and are also good for human health as they provide exercise.

Human-Powered Vehicle Classes

- **Single-rider:** vehicle operated and powered by a single individual
- **Multi-rider:** vehicle operated and powered by two or more individuals
- **Utility:** vehicle used for commuting to work or school, shopping trips, and general transportation

Indonesian Becaks

Becaks or pedicabs, are a popular mode of transportation in Indonesia. There are hundreds of thousands of becaks in many cities. Becaks are three-wheeled vehicles powered by pedals with a passenger seat in the front. Along with being an inexpensive form of transportation, they also provide employment to millions of people. Becaks have, however, been banned from most parts of central Jakarta, the Indonesian capital, because they cause lot of traffic congestion.

Bicycle

The *bicycle* is the most popular human-powered vehicle. It is a two-wheeled vehicle powered by the human leg and foot. Bicycles come in many types according to their function, including the utility bicycle, mountain bicycle, and racing bicycle, among others. The  earliest bicycles were called *velocipedes* and were made from wood. In 1817, the modern bicycle was invented by the Frenchman Baron Karl von Drais.

Rickshaws in Bangladesh

Bangladesh is a country in southern Asia. In Bangladesh, one of the most common forms of transportation is the *rickshaw*. More than 80% of the population use rickshaws as their main mode of short-distance transportation. Dhaka, the capital of Bangladesh, with more than a quarter million rickshaws, is known as the "Land of Rickshaws." Rickshaws provide a pollution-free environment and are a convenient form of transportation. Rickshaws are the main source of income for about five million people in Dhaka.

Countries Going Green

An American environmental economist, Matthew Kahn, did a worldwide survey of eco-friendly cities and countries. Among the 141 countries surveyed, Finland topped the list as the most eco-friendly country, while Ethiopia was the worst. Kahn's survey is based on statistics from the 2006 United Nations Human Development Index and the 2005 Environmental Sustainability Index. Iceland, Norway, Sweden, and Austria were the other top five eco-friendly countries.

Why are countries going green?

The alarming state of global warming is becoming a th reat for all life on Earth. Many countries are making efforts to go green and save the environment. One of the most important steps of going green is the reduction of greenhouse-gas emissions. Using alternative fuels may reduce carbon dioxide emissions from vehicles, homes, and industries. Governments in many countries urge their citizens to use renewable, clean sources of energy such as solar and wind power. Governments also make grants available to encourage people to go green.

Finland at the Top

Finland topped the list of eco-friendly countries, winning high marks for its water and air quality. In 2005, 27.42% of the energy Finland consumed was from renewable sources. This figure is set to increase to 31% by 2010.

Britain Ranked Low

Britain ranked 25th in the survey of eco-friendly countries. The low rank of Britain is due to its large-scale emission of carbon dioxide, which was more than twice the global average. Britain ranked 77th in terms of greenhouse-gas emissions, 41st in terms of air quality, and 15th in terms of water quality. For energy efficiency and use of renewable sources, Britain was a poor 93rd. The survey suggested a lot of cleanup work for Britain.

Reducing Carbon Dioxide Emissions

Germany, Finland, and the Netherlands were the top European Union countries that reduced their carbon dioxide emissions drastically between 2004 and 2005. Reduced emissions of carbon dioxide increased the overall reduction of greenhouse-gas emissions in these countries. Germany reduced carbon dioxide emissions by 2.3%, Finland by 14.6%, and the Netherlands by 2.9%.

Using Renewable Sources

Global energy consumption is estimated to increase 55% by 2030. Population growth, continued urbanization, and economic expansion widely contribute to this increased consumption percentage. Nevertheless, the large-scale use of renewable-energy technologies can easily meet the energy demands many times over.

Did you know?

The Nordic countries are the world leaders in producing as well as using both renewable energy and alternative fuels.

Greener Denmark and Sweden

Denmark and Sweden are countries in northern Europe. Both these countries belong to a region called *Scandinavia*. Denmark and Sweden are industrialized countries and are among the environmentally cleanest countries in the world. They have made deliberate efforts to reduce greenhouse-gas emissions and become environmentally friendly.

Eco-Centric City

Most Danes in the industrialized areas of Denmark ride bicycles as their preferred mode of transportation. Denmark's capital, Copenhagen, is an eco-friendly city. About 32% of Copenhagen's population travel on bicycles daily, 13% of them travel by train, 20% by bus, 3% drive their own vehicles, and the remaining 5% walk. The bicycle riders of Copenhagen make up the highest percentage of human-powered vehicles in any industrialized urban center in the world.

Wind Power in Denmark

Denmark has the second-largest offshore wind farm in the world. It is named Horns Rev. It powers about 150,000 Danish households. Horns Rev is located off the west coast of Denmark's Jutland peninsula, 8 to 12 miles into the North Sea. The wind farm consists of 80 wind turbines and at capacity can generate 160 megawatts of electricity. The turbines produce 150% more electricity than land-based turbines. The wind farm provides about 2% of the total energy consumed in Denmark.

Fossil-Free Electricity

Sweden is one of the leading countries that generate fossil-free electricity. Sweden uses hydropower and nuclear power extensively to produce electricity. About 28% of the country's energy comes from renewable sources, up from 22% in the last decade. Sweden also uses biomass as an energy resource. About 62% of the energy used for heating homes in Sweden comes from biomass.

Did you know?

A Danish company, FLSmidth, has developed a new technology that uses old car tires as an alternative fuel for cement production. This new technology can reduce CO_2 emissions by 46,000 tons per year.

The World's First Oil-Free Country

Sweden is projected to become the world's first oil-free country by 2020 by replacing oil with renewable energy sources. In 1970, about 70% of their energy came from oil. Today, only 30% comes from oil thanks to their efficient use of alternative energy sources.

The World's Solar Thermal Plants: A Case Study

Solar thermal plants generate power from the energy radiated by the sun. Solar energy is an alternative energy resource that helps to fight global warming. Throughout the world, solar thermal plants are installed to increase the use of solar energy. China, Thailand, Malaysia, Saudi Arabia, Rwanda, India, and Mexico are some countries that are developing photovoltaic plants to harness solar energy.

Spain's Solar Gardens

The world's 10 largest photovoltaic parks are known as *solar gardens*. They are located in Spain. Among these, the more important solar gardens are in Beneixama and Jumilla. The solar garden at Jumilla is currently the world's largest and most efficient photovoltaic plant. It consists of 120,000 solar panels and covers an area of 247 acres. The solar park meets the energy requirements of about 20,000 homes. It helps to reduce carbon dioxide emissions by 42,000 tons every year. The solar park of Beneixama is spread in an area of 5,381,955 square feet installed with 100,000 polycrystalline solar energy panels. It can power nearly 12,000 households and reduces CO_2 emissions to approximately 30,000 tons per year. By extending its solar thermal plants, Spain is helping the European Union to meet its target of reducing greenhouse gases by 20% in 2020.

The European Union

The European Union is the leader in photovoltaic plants, followed by the United States and Asia. Eighty percent of the world's photovoltaic plants are installed in the European Union, while 16% are in the United States and 4% in Asia. In the European Union, Germany and Spain are the major producers of solar energy. They are followed by other countries such as Switzerland, Belgium, the Czech Republic, France, Austria, Luxembourg, and the United Kingdom.

Kigali Solaire

Kigali Solaire is the largest solar power plant in Africa. It is located in Kigali, the capital city of Rwanda. The plant is built in an area of about 31,000 square feet and can generate 325,000 kilowatt hours of electricity per year. Kigali Solaire is set to reduce carbon dioxide emissions by 300 tons annually.

North America's Largest Solar-Electric Plant Switched On

The largest solar photovoltaic system is located in North America. The plant is built at Nellis Air Force Base, which occupies a 140-acre area in southern Nevada. The plant is made up of 72,000 solar panels containing nearly six million solar cells. The panels rotate according to the sun's movement to collect solar energy. The plant provides clean energy and meets 30% of the electrical needs of the air base. The plant helps to reduce 24,000 tons of carbon dioxide emissions annually. This is equivalent to emissions from 185,000 cars on the road.

Solar Program in Rizhao, China

Rizhao is a city in northern China. "Rizhao" means *sunshine*. Earlier Rizhao was not energy self-sufficient. The citizens installed solar panels outside their homes and buildings. The photovoltaic solar plants helped to meet energy requirements such as heating homes, lighting, cooking, traffic signals, streetlights, and park lighting. More than 6,000 families in Rizhao use solar ovens in the kitchen. About 99% of homes use solar water heaters. Solar power has helped every home save about $120 on conventional electric heaters. The solar thermal system not only helped them to become self-sufficient in power generation but also improved the lifestyle of the people.

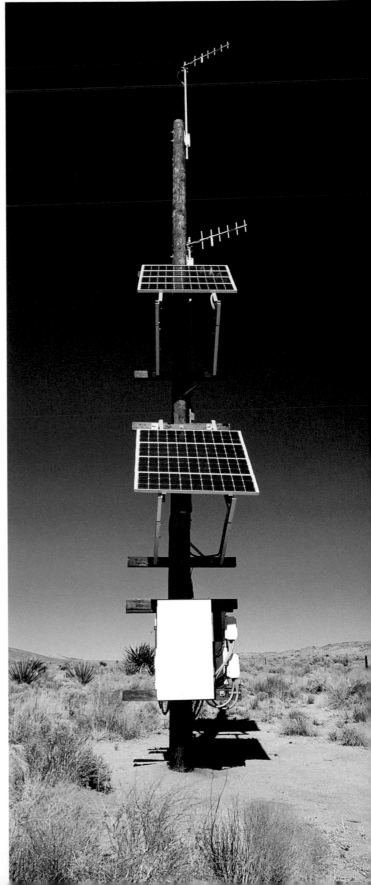

Geothermal Energy in Iceland: A Case Study

Iceland is a European country that lies just below the Arctic Circle. As it is nearer to the Arctic, it has long, cold winters. Iceland is a country of glaciers and steaming hot springs and geysers. So it is popularly known as the "Land of Ice and Fire." Iceland is a hot spot of geothermal activity and has one of the world's largest geothermal power systems. Geothermal power has helped Iceland become a self-sufficient nation for energy needs.

The Geothermal City

Reykjavik is the capital and the largest city in Iceland. Reykjavik means "Smoke Bay" and is named because of the hot springs found there. This city is famous for the world's largest geothermal district heating system, which has been in use since 1930. Reykjavik has five geothermal fields. They are Laugardalur, Elli aárdalur, Seltjarnarnes, Reykir, and Nesjavellir. Geothermal power has helped Reykjavik reduce CO_2 emissions by four million tons per year and has made it one of the cleanest cities in the world.

How does it work?

The geothermal plants in Reykjavik can use both low- and high-water-temperature fields. The low-temperature water is less than 302° F and is located at a depth of 3,280 feet below the ground. The high-temperature water is at about 392° F. It is found at a depth of more than 3,280 feet. The low-temperature water is used for home heating and washing, while the high temperature water is used for electricity generation. Reykjavik has about 800 miles of pipelines to distribute hot water to households.

Meeting Energy Requirements

Iceland has no fossil fuel reserves and is dependent on other countries to meet its energy requirements. About 26% of its electricity comes from geothermal plants, and nearly 85% of homes are heated with geothermal waters. Reykjavik has a population of about 184,000 people. The geothermal plants in Reykjavik use about 2.2 billion cubic feet of water, which meets the energy requirements of 170,000 people.

The Blue Lagoon

Iceland's Grindavik is famous for the Blue Lagoon, which is an artificial hot-water lake. The nearby geothermal power plant at Svartsengi created this lake. The lake contains warm water (104° F) that the geothermal plant releases after generating electricity. The lagoon has been a major tourist destination, as many people bathe in it to help heal skin diseases such as psoriasis.

Facts and Figures

11. The United States ranks second in wind power generation after Germany.
12. The United States is generating 48 billion kilowatt-hours of electricity from wind power in a year, which can power about 4.5 million homes.
13. The world's largest wind turbines are located in Moray Firth in Scotland. Each turbine has blades longer than a football field.
14. Only about 7.5% of U.S. energy comes from renewable resources.
15. The United States will be able to power nearly 40 million homes through renewable resources within 15 years, thus reducing the need for imported oil.
16. One wind turbine powers nearly 300 homes.

1. Americans use about 15 times more energy than people in developing countries do.
2. Ninety percent of the household energy in the United States is used for heating and cooling homes and powering water heaters.
3. A solar water heater can save up to 85% on your electricity bill.
4. The United States had more than 4,000 electric vehicles in March 2002.
5. The largest number of electric vehicles is found in California and the western United States.
6. The United States has more than 20,000 flexible-fuel vehicles.
7. There are nearly one million natural gas vehicles in the world, of which more than 75,000 are found in the United States.
8. One-third of the greenhouse-gas emissions in Australia come from burning fossil fuels.
9. Every Australian consumes about four times more energy than the world average.
10. The earliest windmills were found in Persia, which is now known as Iran.

17. Each of the 500 million automobiles on Earth burns about two gallons of fuel per day on average.

18. Every gallons of fossil fuel releases about 19 pounds of carbon dioxide into the atmosphere when burned.

19. About five million tons of oil produced each year ends up in the ocean.

20. Laptops are energy-efficient and consume 90% less energy than desktops.

21. Refrigerators consume about 7% of U.S. energy.

22. The United States has about 100 million households and five million commercial buildings, which consume one-third of the total energy and contribute 35% of the air pollution.

23. It takes millions of years to create fossil fuels, but it will take less than 50 years to deplete them. Fossil fuels are being depleted about 100,000 times faster than they are being formed.

24. Americans constitute only 5% of the world's population, but they consume about 26% of the world's energy.

Index

Glossary

acid rain: rain containing sulfur dioxide and other pollutants in dissolved form

algae: small, aquatic, rootless plants such as seaweed

alkaline: water or soil having a pH level greater than seven

bacteria: microscopic, single-celled organisms that can cause diseases

carbon dioxide: colorless gas in the Earth's atmosphere that helps in trapping heat close to the Earth

combustion: the process of burning

components: different parts that combine with other parts to make up a whole

composition: a mixture of various parts to form a whole

corrosive: substance that can wear down or dissolve things

current: the flow of electricity through a wire

decompose: to break down and decay

density: thickness or compactness of a substance

ecosystem: a complex community of living things in a physical environment

element: a simple chemical substance that consists of atoms of only one kind

emission: discharge of substances into the air

exhaust: fumes released from a vehicle engine and other machine parts

fermentation: the process of breaking down of complex molecules with the help of a ferment

force: the pushing or pulling of an object to move it

fossil fuel: fuel derived from organic remains, such as petroleum, coal, or natural gas

gap: open space

generator: a machine that produces electricity

geological: relating to geology, earth science

geyser: a natural spring of hot water that sometimes rises suddenly into the air

glacier: a large body of ice that moves very slowly

global warming: an increase in the average temperature of the Earth

greenhouse gas: a gas that traps heat in the Earth's atmosphere

groundwater: fresh water found beneath the surface of the ground

habitat: an environment in which a plant or animal normally lives and grows

heavy metal: metal that is harmful to our health, such as lead or mercury

hot spring: a place where hot water comes up naturally from the ground

hydroelectricity: power generated from the force of rushing water

industrial revolution: period between 1700s and 1800s when power-driven machinery began to replace human-powered tools

livestock: domesticated animals raised for the production of meat or milk

microorganism: a very small organism invisible to the naked eye

model: a miniature representation of something

organic: derived from living things such as plants and animals

ozone: a toxic gas that consists of three atoms of oxygen; a major source of pollution on the Earth

particulate: tiny, solid pieces of material or liquid droplets in the air

petroleum: an oil composed of hydrocarbons that occurs naturally under the Earth's surface

pollutant: a substance that contaminates and pollutes air, water, and land

pulp: a substance beaten or crushed to become soft

radiate: to emit or give out rays or waves of energy

sorghum: cereal that can be made into flour or syrup

thermal: power energy caused by heat

toxic: containing poison

treat: to apply special substances to give a particular quality

turbine: engines or motors in which the pressure of a liquid or gas moves a special wheel around

urban: related to a city or town

volatile organic compound (VOC): a carbon-rich chemical that evaporates at room temperature

waste: unwanted material